David R. Plunket

Address Delivered in the Dining-Hall of Trinity College

Anatiposi

David R. Plunket

Address Delivered in the Dining-Hall of Trinity College

Reprint of the original.

1st Edition 2023 | ISBN: 978-3-38230-166-8

Anatiposi Verlag is an imprint of Outlook Verlagsgesellschaft mbH.

Verlag (Publisher): Outlook Verlag GmbH, Zeilweg 44, 60439 Frankfurt, Deutschland
Vertretungsberechtigt (Authorized to represent): E. Roepke, Zeilweg 44, 60439 Frankfurt, Deutschland
Druck (Print): Books on Demand GmbH, In de Tarpen 42, 22848 Norderstedt, Deutschland

University of Dublin.

COLLEGE HISTORICAL SOCIETY.

ADDRESS

DELIVERED

IN THE DINING-HALL OF TRINITY COLLEGE,

AT THE

First Meeting of the Seventeenth Session,

NOVEMBER 9, 1859.

BY THE AUDITOR,

DAVID R. PLUNKET, A.B.

DUBLIN:

HODGES, SMITH, & CO., GRAFTON-STREET,

BOOKSELLERS TO THE UNIVERSITY.

1859.

EXTRACT FROM THE MINUTES.

THE opening meeting of the Seventeenth Session was held in the Dining Hall, on Wednesday evening, November 9th, 1859. The Chair was taken at 8 o'clock by the Right Hon. Joseph Napier, President of the Society.

Among those on the platform were the Right Hon. the Lord Justice of Appeal; the Right Hon. Baron Greene; the Hon. Justice Hayes; the Right Hon. James Whiteside; the Lord Mayor; Master Brooke; Master Bushe; Sir J. J. Coghill, Bart.; Master Lyle; J. A. Lawson, LL. D., Q. C.; J. H. Otway, Q. C.; A. Gayer, LL. D., Q. C.; Rev. S. Butcher, D. D., Regius Professor of Divinity; Rev. Dr. Moore, S. F. T. C. D.; Rev. Dr. Graves, F. T. C. D.; Rev. Prof. Galbraith, F. T. C. D.; J. E. Walsh, LL. D., Q. C.; E. Sullivan, Q. C.; Rev. W. C. Plunket; T. H. Barton, Esq.; Dr. Shaw, F. T. C. D.; Dr. Ingram, F. T. C. D.; J. A. Wall, Q. C.; J. George, M. P.; Rev. J. W. Stubbs, F. T. C. D.; D. C. Heron, LL. D., Q. C.; J. Anderson, Esq.; C. Otway, P. L. C.; Henry Darley, Q. C.; Wm. Gibson, Esq.; T. Geoghegan, Esq.; Rev. Wm. Greene; Rev. J. Wills, D. D.; J. Ball, Esq.; Josias Smyly, M. D.; J. R. Stewart, Esq.; Dr. Anster, Regius Professor of Civil Law; Rev. G. Sidney Smith, D. D.

The Minutes of the last meeting having been read by the Secretary, the Auditor, Mr. David R. Plunket, delivered the opening Address.

It was moved by the Right Hon. F. Blackburne, Lord Justice of Appeal:—"That the thanks of the Society be given to the Auditor for his Address."

A 2

The Right Hon. James Whiteside, M.P., seconded the motion, which was passed unanimously.

It was moved by J. A. Lawson, LL. D., Q. C.:—" That the Address of the Auditor be printed and circulated at the expense of the Society."

E. Sullivan, Esq., Q. C., seconded the motion, which was carried *nem. con*.

The President then presented the Medals and Certificates to the successful candidates in the following order :—

FOR ORATORY.

Gold Medal, ...	W. E. H. Lecky, A.B.
First Silver Medal, . . .	F. C. Wills.
Second Silver Medal, . .	J. W. Rynd.
Certificates of marked thanks,	A. Houston, A. B.
,, ,,	I. Heazle, A. B., *sch*.

FOR HISTORY.

Gold Medal, ...	C. E. Cartwright, A.B.
Silver Medal, ...	C. W. Benson, A.B.

The Society's Prize for Prose Composition; subject— " Party Government," was awarded to Mr. F. C. Wills.

The Napier Gold Medal (instituted 1859) was awarded to Mr. Edward Gibson, A.B., for the best Essay on "The Future of Italy."

The President shortly addressed the Society, and the meeting separated.

ADDRESS.

It is one of the many pleasant duties of that office with which you have honoured me, that I should, in opening a new session of our Society, review our past labours, and seek to stimulate you to fresh exertions for the future ; and never, I believe, did this duty devolve upon any Auditor under more cheering circumstances. Before, however, proceeding to these particular considerations, it is my intention, in accordance with a series of most imitable precedents, to consider somewhat more generally that object which we profess pre-eminently to pursue in this Society—Eloquence. You need not, however, fear from me a treatise upon Oratory in the abstract. That subject has been so often and so satisfactorily dealt with in all ages, by men of the greatest ability, that I feel convinced that any attempt on my part, in the same direction, would be certain to result only in vague generalities, or bare truisms. The topic which I have selected is circumscribed within much narrower limits ; but is for us, I think, of no less importance. It is—Public Speaking at the present day.

I have chosen this view of the subject, not only because I hoped that it might prove interesting to such an audience as I have this evening the privilege of addressing, but also because its consideration must involve the discussion of questions, on the respective decisions of which depends altogether the value of such a Society as ours ; questions, too, as it seems to me, of the uttermost importance to him who entertains high hopes of some day doing honourably by himself, and well by his country.

Moreover, Gentlemen, I feel convinced, that on this subject most erroneous and confused notions popularly prevail ; for it seems to be very often believed among practical people, that the day is now gone by when Eloquence, or, as it is sometimes rather discourteously termed, " Talk," can avail in anywise with men. This is regarded by some with indifference, as an inevitable social tendency ; by others with complacency, as a notable sign of the increased common sense of the day. From either view of the case, the inference, even when not stated in terms, is irresistible, that the study of Oratory as an art, in such an institution as this Society, is useless, if not something worse. I am not therefore aware of any subject, which, for one holding the position that by your courtesy I now occupy, it could be more pertinent to discuss; and I accept the task with the greater satisfaction, as I am convinced that a fair and practical consideration of the subject will lead to the conclusion that there never was a time in the history of our country, when a nobler opportunity was afforded for the exertions of the Public Speaker.

I think, Gentlemen, that we shall find the truth to be, that while in some of its departments the style of Eloquence has altered in obedience to the changing tastes and circumstances of the times, in its character, as a great social fact, Eloquence has in our day gained in power and importance.

I propose, then, to examine Public Speaking at the present day, successively, in its respective developments in the Senate, on the Platform, in the Pulpit, and at the Bar.

In the first place, then, Public Speaking at the present day, in its political aspect, viz., in the Senate. I think that to any one who has studied the Parliamentary speeches of sixty years ago, or thereabouts, and has impartially compared with them the corresponding productions which are now daily reported in the newspapers, the reflection must have suggested itself, that when this generation shall have given place to another, and our successors come dispassionately to compare the Parliamentary Eloquence of our predecessors with our own; when all the little incidents that to us give intense interest to the simplest statements, and point to many a passing allu-

sion, shall have been forgotten ; when the speeches
of each period shall be read and judged purely
in the light of isolated intellectual efforts, that a ver-
dict will go against this generation; that in powerful
appeal to the reason, in fanciful appeal to the ima-
gination, in fiery appeal to the passions, in sublime
appeal to the primal sensibilities and noblest principles of man's nature,—in almost every attribute
which goes to make up what we call Eloquence,—the
Parliamentary Orators of our day did not approach
to that high standard of excellence which was attained by their predecessors.

This, I think, is the comparative judgment at which
future critics will arrive ; but, on the other hand, I
am far from asserting that the present style of Parliamentary Eloquence has not its peculiar merits,—
merits which, when we consider closely that great
assembly itself, seem more appropriate to its altered
circumstances than those qualities which it has lost.
For those excellencies consist in a business-like pre-
cision of manner, an unexaggerated fairness of statement, and a calm purity of language, which, on
occasion, gathers to a glow of intense earnestness,
that in its simplicity approaches nearly to the sublime. All that I mean to assert is this, that our
age has not produced many great speeches, that can
be compared to the eloquence of sixty years ago.
Are we in this generation likely to behold—is it
possible to conceive—the re-enactment in the new
Houses of Parliament, at Westminster, of such scenes

of sumptuous Eloquence, of absorbing excitement, as accompanied the trial of Warren Hastings, or immediately preceded the Union of 1800 ? I think it is scarcely too much to say, that the generality of Parliamentary Speaking is little above the average of the articles in our leading journals; and that it is only on very rare occasions that it rises to anything that can be fairly called lofty Eloquence And yet I think that when we shall have considered the causes of which this Parliamentary dulness is the necessary result, so far from experiencing unavailing regrets, we shall be filled with feelings of the deepest satisfaction and gratitude.

Now, there is one way of accounting for this on the very face of it: Parliament has no time for any superfluous speaking, because not only has every town and county in the United Kingdom an unquestionable right to have its particular wants supplied by the collective resources of the realm, and its peculiar wrongs redressed by its collective wisdom ; but also, because from that assembly must proceed the policy, that is to sway one-fifth of the world. And thus the ever increasing intricacy of our social system, and the continual extension of our commercial interests, have led to such an accumulation of business details as have rendered it necessary to establish, not only a system of precedents called Rules of the House, but also a very strict etiquette. And the usefulness of these restrictions on any but the most business-like speaking has been found so great, that few are now hardy enough to question their authority.

Again, the effect must be very considerable which is produced on the mind of the orator, when at the moment that he feels himself rising to a burst of eloquence more than usually impassioned, a chilling consciousness comes upon him that every statement made in the heat of debate must appear in fearful integrity in the morning journals, there to be calmly sifted by the cool and reflective mind of the breakfast table critic; and that for every word lightly spoken he shall have to render a terrible account to the pens of a hundred ready writers, who are eagerly awaiting an opportunity for an attack on the party to which he belongs. And this must act upon him with redoubled force when he recollects that at no distant period, he must again appeal to his constituency. This cause of oratorical dulness has, doubtless, operated with much greater effect since the Reform Bill of 1832; for, before that period, many an old Lord or wealthy Commoner had in his power the return of several Members to Parliament. This privilege was often exerted in favour of some young man of oratorical promise, whose first object it was to prove in debate that the discriminating judgment of his patron had not misplaced the trust. Since, however, the great Reform Bill was carried, the power of returning Members has almost entirely passed into the hands of a different and more practical class, who do not so much care that their poli-

tical views should be stated in fine words, as that
their wishes should be carried into effect with as
much rapidity and certainty as possible. But, Gentlemen, there is another cause of the absence in general of good speaking which I think we cannot but
regard with a feeling of anxiety and regret. It arises
from the hollow and insincere professions of prin-
ciple too often made by the members of contending
parties. For, in order that the great parties may have
what is technically called a "good cry," with which
to influence their respective constituencies, they are
in the habit of holding extreme views, and making
exaggerated statements from the hustings and elsewhere, with regard to questions whose true merits
have long since been decided upon by men of enlightenment. When, however, these gentlemen
come to support the same opinions before an assembly so well informed and so fastidious as the House
of Commons, they hesitate to appeal to patriotic and
immutable principles, that accord so ill with the
narrow bigotry of their professed political creed—
well knowing that a glance at "Hansard" is sufficient
to show that their motives are in fact very personal
and unsteady. For views fixed by party vicissitudes
rather than political ethics, are ever inconsistent. I
think there is a curious indication of the existence
of this disease to be found in the terrible edge which
has of late years been set upon that scalpel of Parliamentary practice, personal satire.

This last consideration is not very gratifying to us,
and it has long afforded a fair mark for the sarcasms

of other governments. But, Gentlemen, there is one cause, of which I have not yet spoken, but of which I must now tell you. It is indeed the final cause, for it produces all the others; and, when I think upon it, I am reconciled to every drawback of less importance. This Parliamentary dulness is to us the consequence of a long and enduring peace, founded upon a perfect freedom ;* and other Governments are welcome to their small sneer. It is under the influence of this security and this freedom that has been developed a spirit of commercial energy, and steady, unyielding endurance, that has spread into every corner of the earth an empire of which we can boast, in no lying profession, that its spirit is peace. It is this security and this freedom that have rendered the last shackles of the press unnecessary, and that permit and compel the Government to appeal through a hundred journals to that common sense that is indeed the only tenure of its authority. It is because of this security and this freedom that the nation views with comparative indifference the squabbles of factions and the petty jealousies of party, well knowing that to its own surer keeping is committed the peace and liberty that it holds so dear. Yes, Gentlemen, it is because from year to year, and from age to age, the

---

* " Les Anglais ont considéré l'art de la parole comme tous les talents en genéral, dans le point de vue de l'utilité ; et c'est ce qui doit arriver à tous les peuples, après un temps de répos fondé sur la liberte."—*Madame de Staël, " De l'Eloquence et de la Philosophie des Anglais."*

voice of Eloquence has pleaded throughout this land for liberty,—rousing the energy of the patriot, tempering the zeal of the reformer, appealing alternately to the dauntless courage and the calm moderation of Englishmen, until at last we have arrived at a happy era, when it is no longer necessary to instil into the heart of the nation a love of freedom that is its very life-blood.

Let us not, then, lament that the Parliamentary eloquence that roused our forefathers to deeds of daring seems now to slumber,—the sleep, not of death, but of security. I do believe that there is in the breasts of Englishmen a sober, though intense feeling of patriotism that is too sacred to be lightly spoken of, but to which in hour of need the patriot orator shall appeal with magic power. It is not many months since there was but a suspicion that something else was sought to be relied upon for the safety of the freedom of Englishmen, than their own determination to defend it. " An old Peer" spoke a few eloquent words of trust, and courage, and patriotism. It was but a short speech, after all ; but the heart of England bounded wildly in answer to the appeal.*

But though we can now seldom hope to find in its accustomed place in Parliament that kind of eloquence which once culminated there, let us not therefore hastily infer that the orator's occupation is gone. There are other opportunities demanding his utmost exertions ; for the eloquence that once

* Lord Lyndhurst's speech on the National Defences, July 5, 1859.

flooded the galleries of the House with tears, and set peeresses fainting, may now find itself other and nobler avocations. It may ascend the Pulpit to startle lethargic congregations, to give contentment to the poor, and rest to the weary-hearted ; it may enter the Lecture-room and Assembly-hall to rouse the intellect of the people, slumbering too long,—to advance the great cause of human happiness, to preach an Intellectual Revival to the masses. This is what I have called the Eloquence of the Platform ; and this I conceive to be a noble opportunity for the exertions of the orator. Perhaps some of you may think this scheme novel, far-fetched, and Utopian. Novel it certainly is, but so are the circumstances that have called it forth ; and do not decide that it is altogether far-fetched and Utopian until you have considered it more closely, for it is no crude theory of my own, but the proposal of the best and wisest of Englishmen,—such men as the late Sir Robert Peel, Lord Brougham, and the good Arnold; men who not only advocated the scheme by eloquent precept, but in the midst of pressing and multitudinous employments, found time to labour in it earnestly themselves.

And, indeed, if you consider for a moment or two the condition of the lower orders, the necessity and opportunity for such exertions will at once present themselves. The state of the masses is a consideration on which we seldom suffer our minds to dwell. Now and then it is thrust upon us ; and, as some instance of horrible crime, or lamentable folly, forces itself upon our observation, we put it away again with the remark, that it is strange these things should occur in an age of enlightenment, and with a feeling that we are glad that we, at all events, have nothing to do with such people. Gentlemen, we have everything to do with such people; and if we do not look to it now, our boasted enlightenment may play us a dangerous trick. At this day, the state of the masses is socially and morally miserable and degraded. Even you, Gentlemen, who have made a pleasant excitement of school and college,—even you, with your good things in this life, and perhaps your hope of better things in a life to come,—even you sometimes grumble about the vanity of your pursuits, the finality of your pleasures, and, on the whole, you are inclined to agree with the Hebrew of old, "that man is born to misery." But picture to yourself a darkness through which no pure hope ever beckons, a darkness so thick that it seems as if the very eye of God could not pierce it; imagine souls whose only affinities are with the gin-shop, or sodden, smoky lanes that soil the very sunshine, whose future is work,—a weary dead level of work on to the very horizon, and there only doubt and uncertainty; nothing to-day but to eat and to drink and to work, and to-morrow to die. This is actually the state of tens of thousands of the manufacturing populations of England; and if we do not feel it here with equal force as yet, still, with the growth of our commerce and manufactures, it will grow upon us. Knowledge comes to them just in a sufficient degree to make them fully conscious of their misery ; nor should we feel much surprised at the result. The hard riddle has been proposed to them of well-fed idleness and ill-fed toil; they read that God ordained that those who work should live, but they find that society has reversed the fiat, and that those who work must starve. We cannot, then, I say, much wonder if their notions on political economy are rather vague,—if they regard with bitter hate those classes that, isolated high above them in the upper regions of society, lade them with heavy burdens, grievous to be borne, but will not so much as touch them with the tip of their fingers.

Added to all this, there is here in Ireland a peculiar necessity for our exertions. The hard lot of the lower orders, that in England expresses itself in Socialism and Chartism, has here another form. The history of an old oppression, long since broken up, still dwells in the traditions of the people, and all the sufferings that are inevitable in their position are attributed to the tyranny of the Saxon rule; to it they ascribed every ill that flesh is heir to—their poverty, and even their crime; the blood they spilt was upon its head; and the reward of their own sloth and aversion to change was visited on it. But now, when a long season of prosperity has set in—when our countrymen are no longer indignant that ill-tilled land should yield a scanty harvest, because the harvests are plentiful ; when they are no longer outraged, that crime brings punishment, because crime has almost ceased, they have still the miseries that are inseparable from a working lot ; these, now, they begin to lay on the broad shoulders of Saxon rule. A little knowledge makes the people sensitive to the hardships belonging to their state, and gives them strength and unity, but not wisdom. A generation ago they had been thankful for their present prosperity, because they were ignorant then—they tilled the soil in their strength, and let politics alone. A fighting, blundering, pig-driving, and intensely amiable people, enthusiastic, visionary Young Irelanders strove to shake them up into political life—in vain ; a sensitive imaginative nation, they searched them with the fire of eloquence—in vain ; they spoke of real grievances, for those were the "Penal days," and orators never spoke as they spoke—in vain ; they spread the past before them with its lights and shadows—in vain ; what did they rouse them to ? Here the burning of a farm-house, there a scuffle with the constables—that was all ; ignorance kept them disunited ; in the dark they lost one another. But you have built a school-house in every parish in the last thirty years ; you have taught them to read, and to write too ; you have given them a Press, which makes the cause of crime and anarchy the cause of Ireland, and unites the people in this wretched delusion. Have a care, or the day is coming when the Orator shall speak—not in vain ; when he shall misrepresent, and exaggerate, and inflame—not in vain; when they shall recall the past—not in vain; and the people shall answer with a shout—not in vain.

Gentlemen, it is into these masses of ignorance and discontent that I call upon you to go down, to stir up amongst them a spirit of self-improvement, and give it a safe direction; to raise their moral standard, by branding vice, intemperance, and improvidence with loathing, and by showing the beauty and excellence of morality, of virtue, and of truth; to raise their intellectual standard, by interesting them in scientific and literary pursuits; to break down the prejudices so natural in their circumstances, by expounding the great principles of social progress; to teach our own countrymen that good patriotism can never be opposed to good common sense; and to show them that by self-improvement they may gain a nobler independence than any Young Irelander ever preached, freeing themselves, not from Saxon connexion, but from Saxon superiority; and, finally, to bridge over that chasm that now yawns between the upper and lower classes, by establishing feelings of intellectual sympathy and mutual confidence.

Gentlemen, there are ample opportunities of making the experiment: there is scarcely a town of any importance in these islands that has not a Mechanics' Institute, or an Athenæum, or a Young Men's Society, or some organization of the kind—the result of the people's strong desire to improve themselves—

where you may lecture to audiences that will gladly listen to you. But, perhaps you will say, what effect could *we* produce upon such deeply-rooted prejudices ? I do not, indeed, propose that young men should lecture upon Sociology, or the rights and wrongs of their audience. Such delicate questions must be left to men, who, from their experience and matured wisdom, as well as from their position and character, are calculated to inspire respect, and carry conviction with them. But outside of these there are a hundred questions, in the wide domains of history, of literature, of science, and of art, on which many of you are perfectly capable of lecturing; and, remember, that every such opportunity, rightly taken advantage of, is not only an addition to their stock of knowledge, but actually raises their intellectual standard by so much. Do not, then, shrink from this noble undertaking, because the work seems mighty and the means seem small. I do not, indeed, expect that all the lower orders will be immediately turned from their prejudices and mistakes, by a few lectures delivered here and there; the process must be repeated again and again; and even then it is not so much to the immediate effect that we must look,—it is to the after influence that they will exert on the reading and thinking of the people, for there is an earnest spirit of inquiry abroad amongst them,—they are seeking some means of escape from their ignorance and degradation ; and of this you may be sure, that if you do not avail yourselves of this mode of assisting them, there will be found amongst themselves an abundance of Orators, who, knowing well the passions and prejudices of their audience, will not fail to suggest those short and easy methods of freeing themselves from their miseries,—Revolution and Communism. Nor can you expect that sound books and cheap journals will take your place. When the poor man comes home fagged and weary from a day of unceasing toil, he will scarcely apply himself to root sound views out of deep books, to digest, and compare, and remember ; and as to that class of journals which prevails amongst the people, in nine cases out of ten, instead of rectifying their errors, they will be found to confirm their prejudices, and pander to their passions. This is just the want that the Platform can supply: from it you can present to them sound views, comprised in a short space, and served up in the most interesting and impressive form, combining your lessons with amusement, which is, after all, the most memorable mode of teaching.

Of course, on these occasions you can only address a small section of the classes of which we speak ; still it is the most important section that we thus come at : it is the lower grades of the middle classes, and those of the lower classes who have, by their own independent exertions, raised their intellectual status—men who have won their way up the steep incline of knowledge by steps, cut by themselves, in the hard rock of an over-worked existence. Intellectual culture is not the business of their lives ; it must be had in exchange for hours stolen from a dearly-earned slumber. Do not believe that to these men truth does not come with power. If you ever meet with, or speak to such men, you will find in them an honest pride in their intellectual candour and integrity, and an individual reality of mind, which, I fear, you might often seek for in vain amongst the more conventional, though enlightened upper classes. These are the men that, in times of tranquillity, form the opinions of the masses ; and, in times of revolution, rise high above them to sway with absolute authority.

Gentlemen, I now call upon you solemnly not to neglect this social instrument—The Platform ; greatly powerful, as it is, to educate, to regenerate, to liberate our people. This has been the question of fifty years; it is the question of to-day : others pass and repass, but this of the education of the masses ever holds an uneasy place. We know that the people are rising up around us, a very tide of ignorance and discontent ; strange forms of error move amongst them ; strong, fierce currents of passion stir them ; the growing strength of the people's will gains upon us; and in every lull of political excitement their voice comes like the roar of a far sea. The present state of things cannot last. Thank God ! this system of human machinery and moral degradation cannot last; sooner or later a great change must come social, and, therefore, political. I do believe that it is for us to decide whether this change shall come in stormy revolution or grand constitutional movement. Now, Gentlemen, there is ample opportunity for your exertions ; but if you do not avail yourselves of it now while you can, perhaps the day may come when, in the terror and turmoil of revolution, too long delayed, you may long for a sympathy that now you may kindle if you will; you may then appeal frantically, but in vain, to principles of political wisdom and moderation, which you failed to inculcate while you might—" charming to the deaf adder, that will not hear, charm you never so wisely." Gentlemen, there are great dangers, though we seldom think about them; but there are great hopes too. In the gigantic educational schemes that shall produce more deeply, and, therefore, more safely, learned generations: there are, too, plastic elements in our old constitution, that have brought it safely through many a dangerous crisis, though none, I think, more perilous than this.

It is written in the elder history of that constitution, that when, in the progress of the people from barbarism, the pressure of a social system of degrading villeinage began to be felt, there was found to subsist between the lord and the serf, on the one hand an affectionate sympathy, on the other a respectful gratitude, that led to and made easy that voluntary granting of freedom by the lord to the serf, on which all the after power and glory of England have been built. That was the day of social progress; this is the day of intellectual enlightenment. When the time shall come for a great change, let us be found toiling among the people, in friendly intercourse and sympathy of mind, and then, perhaps, we may accomplish an intellectual regeneration—a mental manumission that shall, with the help of God, prove a second youth to our country.

Gentlemen, I do not think it necessary to dwell, at any length, on Public Speaking at the present day in its two other leading developments. The existence and importance of Eloquence at the Bar seems to be tacitly admitted, even by those who are sceptical about it elsewhere. Important changes, indeed, have of late taken place in many of the principles, and much of the practice of our Courts, but they seem all rather to have a tendency to elevate the style of forensic Eloquence, by simplifying the process of justice, and making it more a matter of common sense.

Pulpit Oratory remains to be considered, and I have come to it last, not as the least important in this age, but as the most obviously important. The flocking after and pursuit of eloquent preachers signifies a want felt by the people, and if the parish church is deserted, it is because mediocrity in preaching has been outgrown, and a higher standard must be had. At the same time, to Pulpit Oratory a literary measure of excellence is less applicable. Bringing the same message to many classes,—the rough-handed peasant, and the highly-refined gentry —to Lazarus and Dives,—it must adapt itself everywhere to its hearers. To thus adapt itself thoroughly

is its perfect excellence. There is but one charac-
teristic, which should be common to all—that is,
earnestness in the preacher; to lose himself in his
subject, to see his subject through his hearers, is,
perhaps, the only comprehensive definition of all
good preaching.

Thus far have I treated Public Speaking at the
present day in its various important developments;
but, before dismissing the subject, I will consider
very shortly one sweeping objection to Eloquence in
all of them. It is one of the many cants of this day,
to contrast the offices of the great doer and the eloquent talker, as utterly and irreconcileably opposed
to each other,—to compare silent individual labour
with what they call contemptuously, "the Orator's
barren harangue." Gentlemen, to this great doer
I would answer thus:—Exert, by all means, the
faculties you have upon whatever silent individual
work ever occurs to you; and it is the labouring
together of thousands of such silent workers that
carries out, and, in fact, composes all the great
movements amongst men. The work of the soldier
who stands patiently in his ranks, and drops where
he stands, is as noble, it may be nobler, than that of
the general who bids him stand fast from a safe hill.
But the general carries away the fame of that fight,
and the world gives him the glory of it, not that his
office is intrinsically noblest, but that it is most
widely important—all important, as it were. The
Orator, too, is a captain amongst men; he shares his

command with the writer and journalist; but, were his action as general as theirs, he would be the most powerful of the three. He marshals the crowd; he directs their work; in the assault upon ignorance and prejudice he beckons them on, and in the defence of truth he leads them. These are his actions; he, too, is a great doer; and that in the highest sense, for he works with a thousand hands, and moves onward with a thousand feet. History is laden with the great deeds of Eloquent Talkers, the annals of England are telling of their power. At the self-same time that in France Mirabeau overturned the most effete monarchy on earth, did not the eloquence of Burke preserve for England that constitutional freedom, of which his speeches are at this day the text-books? Is not the name of Henry Grattan the watch-word of Irish nationality? and shall not the memory of Wilberforce be linked with the rights of equal freedom the wide world over? Gentlemen, I cannot believe that since those days the world has changed so much, that great deeds can no longer be done by Eloquent Talkers.

Gentlemen, if I have at all succeeded in establishing the assertion, which, in the outset of my address I made, you must now agree with me that a power of Public Speaking is at this day as important as it has ever been. I do not think it necessary to go over, for you, the old arguments so often triumphantly maintained, that it is in such institutions as this, and not in solitude, that best may be acquired that power. There is one practical argument, which, under the circumstances, renders the use of any others quite uncalled for; it is the character of the audience that I have this evening addressed. Before me I see a gathering of the members of this Society, amongst whom are the representatives of every honour that this University can bestow. Around me (on this platform) are seated men of all religious denominations, who have attained the highest eminence in every branch of intellectual and professional distinction; the vast majority of them are old members, and they have come down here this evening to testify their approval of that Society whose pleasant social intercourse they once enjoyed, and which for them is linked with the earliest recollections of the practice of those abilities that they have since so nobly developed. This is a strong fact.

Another duty now devolves upon me : it is to tell you of the progress of our Society during the last Session; and not only to rouse our present members to fresh exertions, but also to seek to induce those to join us, who, though qualified by their College standing, have not yet done so.

I do not believe that since this Society returned within the walls of College, it has been in the power of any Auditor to chronicle a Session so altogether successful as that over which we have now to look backwards. Within the last twelve months the list of our members has been increased one-fourth; and on the muster-roll appear the names of twenty Scholars, and a still larger number of Medallists at the Degree Examination. Almost the only losses with which we are threatened are of those whom that unsparing Examination, for the Indian Civil Service, has torn from our ranks. And on the whole, Gentlemen, I think that our sorrow is in this case mitigated when we remember the circumstances which compel them to leave us.

The course laid down for the History Medal Examination of this year was in accordance with the suggestion thrown out in the eloquent address of my predecessor, selected from the annals of our own island; and the answering was most satisfactory. The subject chosen for the Society's composition prize, " Party Government," is eminently calculated to call forth productions which will be read with interest.

Gentlemen, we have no Napier Prize this year, for in its place our President has instituted a yearly Medal, which, at the Society's request, is to be called " The Napier Medal;" and, Sir, you must permit me to observe—and I know that I am but speaking the feeling of the whole Society when I say it—that we gladly accept this opportunity of marking, not only our respect for the great abilities that have won for you your august position, but also our affectionate gratitude for that unwearied kindness that, through years of pressing business, has never ceased to watch our progress,—a kindness to which, more than to any other single cause is attributable, I believe, our present prosperity.

But, Gentlemen, it is in our grand pursuit, the study of Oratory, that our progress has been most decided and unmistakeable. Not only are the marks on which the Gold Medal has this year been obtained most deservedly high, but this has been accomplished under the difficulties of a much raised standard of merit. Again, I have to notice with pleasure the decided tendency of our meetings to partake more of the nature of debates than of opportunities for the exhibition of long set speeches. The style, too, I should say, has less of display, but more of earnest reality about it. This is, I confess, that feature of our progress which I view with the most complete satisfaction ; and if you will allow me, I would add this suggestion, not in the least as dictating a rule, but as a hint,—one I think very likely to counteract the most dangerous tendency of the practice of such a Society as this : I should advise, especially such as are beginners, to avoid what I must take the liberty to call the "*artful dodges*" of rhetoric. What it is most important to acquire, at all events, at first is such confidence as may enable you to speak out simply and strongly your views on any question that may arise. In order to acquire this habit, it is only necessary to speak always on that side of any question which you believe to be the right one, never affecting any excitement which you do not feel, or putting forward an argument in which you do not fully believe. The adoption of any other system is certain to lead, not only to the worst moral and intellectual effects, but also to a vicious and unsatisfactory style of speaking; for there is a strongly marked difference between the argument, the appeal, and the illustration, thrown out by the innate power of a mind thinking upon a truth of which it is fully convinced, and of which it is earnest to convince others, and the same process when attempted by one who has undertaken, right or wrong, to maintain a certain position. I have always observed that such persons find it much easier to deceive themselves, than to deceive an audience.

But, Gentlemen, it is not only that in the competition for our Prizes you may acquire a certain knowledge of History, or fluency of pen, or even a readiness and power in debate, that I would press you to join this Society, but because here you may acquire that other knowledge still more necessary for a successful life: I mean that knowledge of your fellow-men—those habits of hearty social intercourse which make a man an agreeable and prosperous as well as a useful member of society. You cannot gain this knowledge in the home circle, nor yet at school amongst boy-companions. The College Examination Hall and Lecture-room do not admit of it, nor even the pleasant social evenings of College sets. But in our Society every clique is represented: no religious difference excludes, no rancorous party-spirit is admitted. In the honourable contests of manly emulation, mean envy or petty jealousy would not for a moment be tolerated. In the intellectual refinement of our literary pursuits, coarseness and ill-feeling find themselves out of place, and retire abashed. Intimacies are formed, and friendships spring up that bid fair to last with life : for of this much you may be sure, that the friendships formed while the heart is fresh and the affections are warm, are worth all the after-thoughts dictated by the calculations of self-interest. But, Gentlemen, on these subjects I need dwell no longer : to you who are members, descriptions of your past experience are unnecessary ; to you who are members not yet, no description can convey the enjoyments of this Society half so well as you may experience them by joining us. Moreover, Gentlemen, I fear that you may begin to think that this Society is, after all, only a pleasant loitering place to while away an evening or to meet your friends ; and I confess, as I turn from the discussion of the great questions that we have just now considered to review the past Session of this Society, the contrast comes upon me with a feeling of rest and relaxation ; for, though those subjects are very noble in themselves,—though they are fraught with great thoughts and high hopes,—though I believe that to the brave heart and strong will the struggles of life are not so difficult as we grapple with them,—though I doubt not that many an eminence that now seems cloud-capped and impracticable grows less and less formidable as we ap-

proach it, still these great questions somehow suggest
the programme of a future of unceasing toil and
varying fortunes,—of much good to be done, and but
a short, weak life to do it in,—of much wrong to be
undone, with fierce, unyielding antagonists in the
struggle. How much, too, of disappointment and
disaster before we can hope to do anything by which
to be remembered!—I say, when I turn from this
scene of struggle in the future, to review our calm
and happy labours now, it is with a feeling of un-
mixed satisfaction. Do not, however, believe that
this feeling is akin to faint-heartedness or feeble de-
spondency. I believe that there is no man so much
to be pitied as the man who, having ability, wants
energy; no life so miserable as a life without an
object. It is just because I believe this Society is
the best means for providing you with both one and
the other that I would press you to join it; because
I am sure, that though it is with a feeling of deep
regret that, one by one, we are obliged to leave it, it
is with a feeling, too, that we are men the better pre-
pared for what is to follow.

There is, indeed, but one responsibility, I know
of, that you incur on entering our guild: it is, to be
patriotic Irishmen. This Society is now in its nine-
tieth year. Called into being at first at the moment
when the spirit of an awakening freedom and a new-
born nationality began to breathe upon this land, it
has watched that freedom's progress,—tenderly
nursed that nationality. For ninety years it has sent

forth the best and greatest Irishmen.—Gentlemen, as
I speak these words, great memories come thick upon
me. This Society had existed for scarcely twelve
short years when Ireland was roused from ages of
torpor and slavery, and a people of serfs became in
one day a nation of freemen ; and if you ask me how
this was accomplished, I answer—pre-eminently by
the Eloquence sent forth from this Society : and if I
am to say what guarded that freedom and that independence well and long, and when that freedom fell
and that independence was extinguished in the ig-
nominy and despair of the nation,—what it was mitigated the disaster and half effaced the shame,—I must
answer again—it was the Eloquence sent forth by this
Society. And, as the mind passes on over years and
years of our country's oppression, and suffering, and
sin, what was it that still guarded her interests and
pleaded her cause ? I must answer still—it was the
Eloquence sent forth by this Society. And when
the Emancipation had at last been carried, and that
great justice had been done, what was it that, through
times of plague, of rebellion, of famine, ever held
forth hope and comfort, and what at last has helped
to win for Ireland peace, prosperity, and plenty ? I
answer still—it was the Eloquence sent forth by this
Society. Finally, if I am asked what it is that at this
day reflects the ancient fame of Ireland in the British
Senate, brings back the bygone glory of her Bar, and
makes the old Halls ring again, I answer—it is the
Eloquence sent forth by this Society. And we, young

men—what have we to do with this? It is a grand position that we stand in. Behind us stretches away the history of our country, over ages of sorrow and oppression; it brightens as it approaches the present; and the future is full of hope and promise. In the day of Ireland's sore distress the men sent forth from this Society did not fail their country ; shall it be said that in the hour of her prosperity we were found wanting?

Gentlemen, these are the great thoughts by which I would seek to rouse you, my fellow-members, to renewed exertions ; these are the inducements that I would hold out to those who have not yet joined us to do so now. I have no others to offer : I desire to offer no others ; for if you are not roused by ambition,—if you care not for friendship or good fellowship,—if you are cold to patriotism, I have no wish that you should become of us.

My task, Sir, is almost done ; but one short duty remains,—short, but most difficult: it is to thank you,—you, Sir, and those other distinguished men who have come down here this evening,—on the part of the Society, for patronizing us,—on my own part, for the consideration with which you have heard the crudenesses, it may be the impertinences, of a very young man. I must thank you all, Gentlemen, for your tolerance during so long a trial ; but, my fellow-members, when I come to thank you, I have no words to do it with. To return thanks for a single favour is a difficult thing,—to return thanks

c

for a multitude is impossible; and now, on this night of your crowning kindness, I have no words to thank you with; I shall not attempt it. I shall ask you one favour more: it is that you will believe that all I have now said, I have not said merely for oratorical effect, or only to fill up the Address which it was my duty to deliver. I have chosen very practical subjects; I have sought to treat them very practically; and I now ask you individually to take them home practically to yourselves: for this is the hope that I would seek to rouse in the hearts of all of us, that, if Providence should spare us, perhaps in the evening of our lives we may enjoy that highest human happiness, an approving conscience, and the gratitude of our fellowmen; that, when our race is almost run, we may perhaps hear the generation of Irishmen, rising up to take our place, declare that the men who at this day went forth from this Society were not the altogether unworthy successors of the Members of the old Historical.

APPENDIX.

College Historical Society.

MDCCCLIX.

FOUNDED 1745. REVIVED 1848.

Patron:

	ELECTED.
THE LORD PRIMATE, ...	1848

President:

| THE RIGHT HON. JOSEPH NAPIER, LL. D. . . . . | 1854 |

Vice-Presidents:

GEORGE ALEXANDER HAMILTON, ESQ.	1843
RIGHT HON. F. SHAW, Recorder of Dublin, ...	1843
RIGHT HON. F. BLACKBURNE, Lord Justice of Appeal, ...	1846
RIGHT HON. M. BRADY, Lord Chancellor of Ireland, ...	1846
RIGHT HON. T. LEFROY, Chief Justice of Queen's Bench, ...	1846
RIGHT HON. PHILIP CECIL CRAMPTON, ...	1847
RIGHT HON. T. B. C. SMITH, Master of the Rolls, ...	1848
THE EARL OF ROSSE, ...	1849
SIR ARCHIBALD ALISON, BART., D. C. L., F. R. S.	1851
RIGHT REV. R. DALY, Lord Bishop of Cashel, &c.	1851
RIGHT HON. DAVID R. PIGOT, Chief Baron of the Exchequer, . . .	1851
RIGHT HON. JAMES WHITESIDE, Q. C., M. P.	1857
JOHN KELLS INGRAM, ESQ., LL. D., F. T. C. D.	1857
ISAAC BUTT, ESQ., LL. D., Q. C., M. P.	1858
JOHN TOLEKEN, ESQ., M. D., S. F. T. C. D.	1859

OFFICERS FOR THE SESSION, 1859-60.

Auditor:

DAVID ROBERT PLUNKET, A. B.

Treasurer:

SAMUEL LEE ANDERSON, A. B.

Secretary:

JAMES WALSH, *sch.*, A. B.

Librarian:

FREEMAN C. WILLS, A. B.

GENERAL COMMITTEE.

Ex-Officio Members.	*Ordinary Members.*
THE PRESIDENT.	HENRY STEWART, A. B.
THE JUNIOR DEAN.	ARTHUR WILSON, *sch.*, A. B.
THE EX-AUDITOR.	W. E. H. LECKY, A. B.
THE AUDITOR.	JOHN R. GARSTIN, A. B.
THE TREASURER.	JAMES W. RYND, A. B.
THE SECRETARY.	
THE LIBRARIAN.	

LIBRARY COMMITTEE.

Ex-Officio Members.	*Ordinary Members.*
THE AUDITOR.	JOHN RIBTON GARSTIN, A. B.
THE SECRETARY.	C. CARTWRIGHT, A. B.
THE LIBRARIAN.	W. D. A. BABINGTON, A. B.
	W. BOURKE, A. B.

MEMBERS OF THE SOCIETY, 1858-59,

ARRANGED IN ORDER OF SENIORITY.

———◆———

Honorary Members: The Fellows of T. C. D., and the Members of the Oxford and Cambridge Unions.

1. William Bradford, *sch.*, A. B., *Ex-Auditor.*
2. George Arthur Waller, A. B.
3. John Ribton Garstin, A. B., *Librarian.*
4. Hon. H. Leeson, *sch.*, *soc. com.*, A. B.
5. Thomas William Snagg, A. B.
6. Edward Gibson, A. B., *Auditor.*
7. Isaac Bond, A. B., *Ex-Secretary.*
8. David Robert Plunket, A. B.
9. John Boxwell, *sch.*, A. B.
10. Robert Daniell, A. B.
11. William Chessborough le Poer Kennedy, A. B., *Ex-Librarian.*
12. Samuel Lee Anderson, A. B.
13. Walter M. Bourke, A. B.
14. Thomas George Dudley, *sch.*, A. B., *Ex-Secretary.*
15. Arthur Wilson, *sch.*, A. B., *Treasurer.*
16. Conway Edward Cartwright, A. B.
17. Raymond d'Andemar Orpen, A. B.
18. William Cooper, A. B.
19. Thomas Wingfield Webber, A. B.
20. Henry Stewart, A. B., *Secretary.*
21. Richard Creed, *soc. com.*
22. William Edward Hartpole Leckey, *soc. com.*, A. B.
23. Wm. John Napier, *soc. com.*, A. B.
24. Freeman Crofts Wills.
25. Joseph B. Grant, A. B.
26. John Pentland Mahaffy, *sch.*
27. Arthur Cecil Lillingston.
28. Matthew Saunders Greene.
29. Andrew Craig Robinson.
30. Clement Richardson, A. B.
31. John Woodroofe, *sch.*, A. B.
32. William Sherlock.
33. James William Rynd.
34. Terence Michael Dolan, A. B.
35. David C. Cochrane, A. B.
36. Richard William Enraght.
37. Arthur Houston, A. B.
38. Charles William Benson, A. B.
39. John Blake Kilkelly.
40. Robert William Buckley.
41. William Carroll, A. B.
42. John S. Leatham, *sch.*, A. B.
43. John Vesey Nugent, *soc. com.*
44. Henry J. Moses.
45. John Woollaston Mainwaring.
46. William D'Alton Babington, *soc. com.*, A. B.
47. John Fallon, *n. f. sch.*, A. B.
48. Anthony Traill, *sch.*
49. Arthur John Booth, *soc. com.*
50. John J. Digges La Touche, A. B.
51. Charles Echlin.
52. Gerald Fitzgibbon, *sch.*
53. William Power.

54. William Shaw Darley, *sch.*
55. James Walsh, *sch.*, A. B.
56. Hussey Burgh Macartney.
57. John James Browne, *sch.*
58. James Lowry Whittle.
59. Lucas Burnet Blacker King, A. B.
60. Isaac Stamers Heazle, *sch.*, A. B.
61. George Keys.
62. John W. Chambers, *sch.*, A. B.
63. Robert Keith Arbuthnot, *soc. com.*
64. John Gifford Jacob.
65. Archibald Henry Hamilton.
66. Francis William Kirkpatrick.
67. Henry Lissignol Dobree.
68. Edward Haughton, A. B., M. D.

69. John Newenham Hoare, *sch.*
70. Thomas William Bell, *n. f. sch.*
71. John Cotter Wood, *soc. com.*
72. John M'Grorty.
73. Guy Alfred Thompson.
74. Goddard Richards Purefoy Colles.
75. Michael Browne, A. B.
76. Richard E. Shakleton, *sch.*, A. B.
77. J. MacDowell.
78. Samuel Radcliffe.
79. Langlois Lefroy, *soc. com.*, A. B.
80. George Hamilton King.
81. John Gray.
82. T. W. Banks.

EXAMINATION FOR MEDALS IN HISTORY.

Examiners:

EDWARD GIBSON, A. B., First Senior Moderator in History, Political Science, and English Literature.

ARTHUR HOUSTON, A. B., Senior Moderator in History, Political Science, and English Literature.

ARTHUR WILSON, A. B., First Senior Moderator in History, Political Science, and English Literature.

Mr. GIBSON.

I.—What laws regulated the succession to principalities and private property respectively in Ireland before 1172? Mr. Hallam mentions a remedy which was sometimes attempted to prevent disorders on the death of a chief?

II. Mention the date and enactments of the Statutes of Kilkenny. How far does Sir John Davies think they were intended to extend? Who was Lord Deputy at that time?

III.—1. Mr. Froude states two causes for the decline of the authority of the Norman leaders in Ireland?

2. Mention the two expedients by either of which the English Government could be maintained, indicating that which Mr. Froude says was exclusively adopted.

IV.—Mention the date and provisions of Poyning's Law. By what article is it peculiarly known?

V.—Write short notes on—

       1. John de Courcy, Earl of Ulster.

       2. Lambert Simnel.

       3. Silken Thomas.

       4. Sir Arthur Gray.

Mr. HOUSTON.

I.—1. What were the most important measures passed by the first Parliament held in Ireland during the Government of Strafford?

2. Mention some of the chief grievances complained of by the Irish Parliament in their accusation against that nobleman.

II.—Give some account of the proceedings instituted by the Commons with respect to the University of Dublin soon after his fall.

III.—Enumerate the principal causes which led to the Rebellion of 1641.

IV.—Trace briefly the connexion of the following individuals with the Irish history of this period :—

> Edward Somerset, Earl of Glamorgan.
> Touchet, Earl of Castlehaven.
> Rinunccini.

V.—Narrate in detail the events of Cromwell's Irish campaign.

Mr. Wilson.

I.—Give a short account of the campaign of 1691.

II.—Trace historically the connexion between the British and Irish Parliaments from the Revolution to 1782.

III.—Describe the proceedings with respect to the Regency in 1789.

IV.—Who were the principal leaders in the Rebellion of 1798? What foreign attempt was made to assist that Rebellion ?

V.—State the chief provisions of the Act of Settlement (1660), the Treaty of Limerick, and the Act of Union.

This book is given special protection for the reason indicated below:

Autograph	Giftbook
Association	Illustration
Condition	Miniature book
Cost	Original binding or covers
Edition	Presentation
Fine binding	Scarcity
Format	Subject

L82—5M—9-64—84330-K